AF673517

THE DEAD MAN

Living with Dying

A Tale of Emotions and Unspoken Realities

First published by Ranveer Singh 2025

Copyright © 2025 by The Dead Man

All rights reserved. No part of this publication may be reproduced, stored or transmitted in any form or by any means, electronic, mechanical, photocopying, recording, scanning, or otherwise without written permission from the publisher. It is illegal to copy this book, post it to a website, or distribute it by any other means without permission.

This novel is entirely a work of fiction. The names, characters and incidents portrayed in it are the work of the author's imagination. Any resemblance to actual persons, living or dead, events or localities is entirely coincidental.

The Dead Man asserts the moral right to be identified as the author of this work.

ISBN-EPUB: 978-93-342-0124-6

ISBN-PAPERBACK: 978-93-343-2795-3

Copyright Registration Number: LD-20250165853

First edition

ISBN: 978-93-343-2795-3

This book was professionally typeset on Reedsy.
Find out more at reedsy.com

Contents

Introduction

In the quiet moments when darkness settles, and the weight of the world feels too heavy, I find solace in this diary—*Living with Dying*. The title is more than just words; it reflects the delicate dance between life and the inevitable end we all face. It symbolizes vulnerability and the raw emotions that stir within when confronting life's most profound truths.

Through these pages, I'll weave stories both untold and yet to unfold—whispers of my soul, fragments of a journey weighed down by tears, regret, and moments of disbelief. Here, I'll confront the grief that shadows my heart, the anger that erupts like violent storms, and the sadness that often feels too heavy to bear. These are the thoughts I can't always share with others, and sometimes not even with myself.

Writing them down won't erase the pain, but perhaps it will offer glimpses of understanding—a path through the darkness. Under the pen name *The Dead Man,* this diary becomes a sacred space for my deepest reflections. It's a sanctuary where I seek to understand my existence, find meaning in fleeting moments, and connect with the essence of life beneath the surface of everyday routine.

Even if these pages remain unread by another soul, they will hold the weight of my heart's confessions. In *Living with Dying,* I embrace the truth that to truly live, we must confront the shadows lingering at the edge of our existence. This is my journey—these are fragments of a life lived in the shadow of mortality.

.

The Dead Man.

One

Echoes of Solitude: A Tale of redemption and Love

Prologue

Do you know what it's like to live in solitude? No friends, no companions, no enemies, no one to praise you, and no one to criticize you—just you and your loneliness.

In the vast expanse of life, there are moments when darkness grips the heart so tightly that even the brightest day feels like an eternal night. For Arjun, this darkness was not just a passing cloud but a storm that had settled in his soul. His past was a landscape of shattered dreams and betrayals, leaving him hollow, with a heart that trusted no one and a mind that viewed the world as an enemy.

It all started with a betrayal so deep that it scarred him for life. Someone he had trusted with his very essence had broken that trust, leaving him in a chasm of despair. His friends drifted away, his ambitions crumbled, and what was once a vibrant personality turned into a fortress of solitude. The boy who once believed in love and friendship now saw every hand extended towards him as a potential dagger.

At some point in life, we all find ourselves alone, sometimes on the outside, sometimes deep within. Arjun, the protagonist of this story, experienced such a phase when he was in the 10th grade. He had a friend, Divya—at least, that's what he thought. They were close, sharing their days and nights with the usual banter of good friends. But one day, everything changed. Without a fight, without an argument, Divya suddenly turned cold. Overnight, their friendship was replaced by silence. Arjun couldn't understand what went wrong. He searched for answers—not for a day, or a week, or even a month, but for an entire year. When the year ended, he gave up—not because he was tired of Divya, but because he was exhausted from chasing someone who didn't want to be found.

This experience left Arjun with scars. He fell into a deep depression, disgusted with himself for pushing everyone away. He turned friends into enemies and his life into a series of lonely, bitter days. But amidst all that loneliness, Arjun found a strange comfort. Being alone wasn't as bad as it seemed, but the disdainful looks he received from others were unbearable. Still, he managed to get by—until the memories began to haunt him.

Memories are like the ocean; no matter how far you run, they always find you. They cling to you, as innocent as a child who just wants to be held. But there's a strange solace in embracing them. When the tears fall, when those memories wash over you like a gentle rain, the weight on your heart lifts—if only for a moment.

Part I: The Past

Two years passed. Arjun was alone, content in his solitude, angry at the world. To others, he appeared as an egoistic, bitter person.

Then, one day, in the midst of his grey existence, a spark appeared. Her name was Tanu. She was everything that Arjun was not—bright, optimistic, and full of life. She had an energy that could light up the darkest corners of the earth, but even she couldn't see the shadows that lurked in Arjun's soul.

Their first encounter was unremarkable, just two strangers crossing paths. Arjun, lost in his thoughts, barely noticed her, but Tanu felt an inexplicable pull towards him. It wasn't love at first sight, nor was it pity. It was something deeper, something primal—a need to heal the wounded.

Arjun knew everyone in his class, at least by face and name, because it amused him to know who talked behind his back. But

Tanu was new, and honestly, he wasn't interested. He mocked her silently—don't ask why; it just felt like something to do. But her smile was different, something that stood out. She quickly became everyone's favorite, both among students and teachers. She had a habit of wasting money on chocolates, not for herself, but to share with others. Arjun missed out on those chocolates since he was often absent. Not that he cared.

Tanu was not one to give up easily. She sensed the pain in Arjun's eyes, the kind that spoke of a thousand untold stories. She started striking up conversations with him, gently pushing past the walls he had erected. At first, Arjun was dismissive, even cold, but Tanu's warmth was relentless. She would sit at his table, talk about the little things in life, and slowly, the fortress began to crack.

Arjun's business studies were weak, so he joined extra classes. Some other students joined too, including Tanu. She asked him for his notes once, saying the teacher had told her to. Arjun gave them to her, and for the first time in a long while, he felt something different—something good.

Days passed, and Arjun and Tanu became friends. They started staying back after classes, spending time together in the evenings. They grew close—very close. Arjun was happy, but his past haunted him. What if Tanu turned out like Divya? What if she started hating him too? Despite his fears, Arjun was happier than he had been in years. His image in the coaching center began to change, thanks to Tanu. Where once he saw hatred and enmity in everyone's eyes, he now saw warmth and acceptance. People started talking to him, and for the first time in a long while, he wasn't haunted by memories or loneliness. It was all because of her.

Arjun's birthday came around—normally a day he didn't care for—but Tanu called and asked him to come to the coaching center. He didn't know why, but when he got there, a surprise party was waiting for him. A surprise party—for him? That was the first thought that crossed his mind. No one had ever done anything like that for him before. Arjun almost broke down but managed to hold it together. It was the best birthday he'd ever had.

A few months later, on October 22nd, Tanu confessed that she liked Arjun. He was about to say yes out of sheer happiness, but then that fear reappeared—the fear of being left alone, the fear of being abandoned. Arjun asked for time, and Tanu never brought it up again—not in chats, not on calls, not even in person. Three months passed, and Arjun couldn't stop thinking about it. His mind wouldn't let it go. So, he proposed to her, thinking that even if the worst happened, he'd end up where he was three years ago. It was one of the happiest moments of his life, maybe the happiest.

But it didn't last. A year and a half later, something happened that made Tanu's family find out about them. Her family liked Arjun, but only as a friend. And there it was again—that fear, standing in front of him, laughing, asking him, "*What now?*" Religion, caste, society—they were all standing in their way. Tanu was ready to fight the world for them, but she looked so weak, so helpless against her own family. They decided to step back, to meet less, and to focus on their goals. They promised that if they reached a certain point in their lives, they'd try to convince their families. Otherwise, they'd let it go.

And so, Arjun and Tanu drifted into a long-distance relationship. One and a half more year passed, making their relationship three years old—but wounded.

As the last rays of the setting sun dipped below the horizon, Arjun stood alone at the cliff's edge, the cold wind tugging at his clothes. The memories of Tanu were like echoes in the wind, haunting yet comforting in their familiarity. He had spent so long clinging to the past, to the pain and the love intertwined. But in that moment, as the darkness began to envelop the sky, he realized that holding on was only tearing him apart. The world had changed, and perhaps it was time for him to change too.

Part II: The New Beginning

The dawn broke gently, painting the sky with hues of pink and gold. Arjun felt the warmth of the new day on his face as he opened his eyes, the weight of yesterday lifting from his shoulders. He wasn't the same person who had stood on that cliff the night before. Something had shifted within him, like the first breath of spring after a long winter. The past was still a part of him, but it no longer defined him. As he took his first step into the day, it felt like the first step into a new life.

In a new city, Arjun struggled with the remnants of his past.

The memories of Divya and the unresolved issues with Tanu lingered like shadows. He had built walls around his heart, believing it was the only way to protect himself. Every new face was a potential threat, every smile a hidden dagger.

Despite the distance and the complications, Tanu remained in Arjun's life. They were no longer physically together, but their bond had not broken. They talked on the phone, exchanged messages, and occasionally met when circumstances allowed. But the weight of their situation was always there, a constant reminder of what they couldn't have.

Tanu wasn't just another girl. She had her own battles, her own scars. But she saw something in Arjun—a spark of the person he used to be, the person he could become again. She didn't push him to open up; she simply offered her friendship, her companionship.

Slowly, Arjun began to lower his defenses. He shared bits and pieces of his past with Tanu, and in return, she shared her own. They found solace in each other's company, a safe haven from the world that had hurt them both.

The change was subtle at first. Arjun began to look forward to their meetings, though he would never admit it. He found himself thinking about her smile, the way she laughed, the stories she told. She was becoming a part of his routine, a small sliver of light that he didn't want to let go of.

But the past is a powerful force, and it wasn't long before it tried to reclaim him. One night, haunted by memories, Arjun lashed out at Tanu. He told her to leave, that he didn't need her, that she was just like everyone else—someone who would eventually hurt him. Tanu was hurt, but she didn't leave. She saw through the anger, understood that it was fear speaking, not Arjun.

The next day, she came back, acting as if nothing had happened. This time, Arjun broke down. He confessed his fears, his mistrust, his belief that the world was out to get him. Tanu listened, her heart breaking for the boy who had been hurt so deeply that he had forgotten how to live.

One evening, as they sat by the lake during one of their rare meetings, Tanu asked Arjun about his dreams. It was a simple question, but it stirred something deep within him. He realized that he had stopped dreaming a long time ago, buried his hopes under layers of pain and resentment.

With Tanu's support, Arjun began to rediscover himself. He started pursuing his passions, things he had given up on when he lost faith in the world. Tanu encouraged him every step of the way, her belief in him unwavering, even from afar.

Instead, Tanu took his hand and looked him in the eyes, even if it was through the screen. *"Arjun, I'm not going anywhere,"* she said. *"We'll face whatever comes together."*

Her words were a lifeline, pulling Arjun out of the darkness that threatened to consume him. For the first time in years, he allowed himself to believe in the possibility of happiness.

For the first time in years, Arjun allowed himself to be vulnerable. He shared the story of his past, the betrayal that had destroyed him, the loneliness that had become his identity. Tanu didn't try to offer solutions; she simply held his hand and let him pour out his pain.

Over time, Tanu helped Arjun rebuild himself, piece by piece. She didn't magically cure his depression, but she gave him the strength to face it. She showed him that not everyone was out to hurt him, that there were still people in the world who cared, who loved without expecting anything in return.

Arjun began to trust again, first in Tanu, then in himself. The fortress around his heart crumbled, and though the scars remained, they no longer defined him. He learned to live with his pain, to accept that it was a part of him but not all of him. He found joy in the little things—reading a good book, taking a walk in the park, spending time with Tanu.

Their relationship wasn't a fairy tale. There were days when the darkness returned, days when Arjun struggled to see the light. But Tanu was always there, a constant reminder that even the darkest night ends with a sunrise.

In the end, Arjun realized that the world wasn't his enemy. It was a place full of both good and bad, of pain and healing. And though he would never forget the wounds of his past, he had found someone who made the journey worthwhile. With Tanu by his side, Arjun faced the world not as a broken man, but as someone who had been shattered and rebuilt, stronger and more resilient than before.

Epilogue

Arjun's story is one of profound transformation, from a young man crippled by the weight of his past to someone who learns to embrace the present and look forward to the future. Through his experiences with Divya and Tanu, he discovered truths about himself and the nature of love that shaped him into who he is today.

What did Arjun learn from all this? That love doesn't always mean holding onto someone forever; it's about recognizing the moments shared and understanding one's own worth. He learned that love isn't about possession but about the connection that touches our souls, even if it's fleeting. In his journey with Tanu, Arjun found that true love allows us to live fully, to experience joy and pain with equal acceptance, and to grow from both. Arjun and Tanu shared beautiful moments, creating memories that would last a lifetime. And though Arjun's fear might have won in the end, he wasn't sad this time. He didn't hate or blame himself.

Arjun's story isn't just a story; it's an essential part of his life. When he looks back, he doesn't see three more years wasted; he's happy because he lived those years. He lived them for Tanu, and after that, he lived for himself, just the way he should have always lived. Arjun realized that he had wasted a lot of time being depressed, dwelling on things that weren't important, things that never really mattered. But now, he's happier—happier than he's ever been.

Arjun's journey teaches us that love is more than just a feeling; it's a journey of self-discovery and growth. It's about embracing the good and the bad, the joy and the pain, and finding peace within ourselves. Arjun found that true love allows us to live fully, to experience life with all its complexities, and to grow from every experience. In the end, he learned that love, in all its forms, is a guiding light through the shadows of our past.

So, Tanu, what have we learned?

-The Dead Man

Two

The Silent Festival

Part I: A Day Unforgotten

March 8, 2024. Shivaratri. For most, it was just another day, but for Rohan, it became a moment that would forever be etched into his memory. He wasn't someone who easily let things go; small moments that slipped by unnoticed by others had a way of tugging at his heart. Today was no exception.

Rohan left his house that morning with his usual optimism, heading to his DISHA coaching center for his classes. He had been part of a close-knit trio—He, Priya, and Naina—inseparable for years. They shared every secret, every laugh, every tear. But lately, something had shifted. Naina had started dating Kabir, a guy from their coaching center. It had been just a month, but already, it seemed like Naina's world had begun to revolve around him.

When Rohan reached the coaching center, he was surprised to find it deserted. The usual buzz of students, the chatter, the noise—all gone. The doors were locked, and an eerie silence hung in the air. Confused, he called Kabir. After a few rings, Kabir picked up, his voice casual and relaxed.

"Oh hey, Rohan! Didn't you know? It's a holiday because of Shivaratri. Coaching is closed today."

Rohan's heart sank, his chest tightening. *"Didn't Naina tell you?"* Kabir's words felt innocent enough, but they cut deep, like a knife slipping between ribs.

Rohan stayed silent for a moment. No, Naina hadn't told him. But she had told Kabir. It seemed like a small thing, but to Rohan, it felt like the ground shifting beneath him—a silent tremor in the friendship he had once thought unshakeable.

"Oh, I guess she forgot," he forced a laugh, masking his disappointment with strained cheerfulness.

After hanging up, Rohan decided to call Naina. The phone rang longer than usual before she picked up, her voice cheerful, and in the background, he heard Priya's laughter—she was with Naina.

"Hey, Rohan!" she greeted brightly.

Rohan swallowed hard before responding. *"You didn't tell me about the coaching holiday today."*

There was a brief pause, barely noticeable, but enough. *"Oh,*

I'm so sorry, Rohan," Naina apologized, her voice tinged with guilt. *"I meant to tell you when I was talking to Kabir last night, but I must have forgotten. I'm really sorry."*

Rohan wanted to believe her, wanted to brush it off as an innocent mistake. But the sting of being forgotten stayed with him. It wasn't just the holiday—it was what it represented. The shift, the change, the realization that maybe, just maybe, he wasn't as important as he used to be.

"It's fine, don't worry about it," he replied quickly, not trusting his voice to hide the crack forming in his heart.

Instead of going home, Rohan found himself sitting in the empty coaching center. The silence around him felt suffocating. He stared at the dusty chalkboards, the rows of empty chairs, and the abandoned notes scribbled on desks. A place once filled with memories now felt like a hollow shell. He waited for Naina to call him back, to realize how much she had hurt him, but the phone stayed silent. Each passing second deepened the ache in his chest.

He blinked back the tears threatening to spill, his frustration bubbling up. Why did something so small hurt so much? Why did it feel like the ground had shifted beneath him?

Deep down, he knew it wasn't about Shivaratri or the forgotten message. It was about everything that came with it—the changes, the distance, the fear of being left behind. The trio, once inseparable, now had cracks—tiny fractures that felt like they might tear it apart.

He sat there for what felt like hours, lost in his thoughts, until the weight of his sadness became unbearable. Wiping away the last of his tears, he finally made his way home, each step heavier than the last.

When he walked in, his mother noticed the storm cloud over his usually bright demeanor.

"Everything okay, Rohan?" she asked gently.

He nodded, brushing her off as he made his way to his room. He didn't want to talk, didn't want to explain the ache in his heart. Lying on his bed, he stared at the ceiling, willing himself not to cry again. He felt weak, foolish even, but the pain lingered, refusing to be ignored.

For the rest of the day, Rohan kept to himself, hiding in the silence of his room. He buried the incident deep, pushing it to the back of his mind, but it had already carved a permanent place in his heart—a reminder of the day when everything changed.

Part II: Moving Forward

In the weeks that followed, Rohan tried to move past what had happened. He smiled when needed, laughed when appropriate, but a distance now separated him from his two best friends. He began spending more time alone, finding comfort in his books, his thoughts. Naina and Priya noticed, but they didn't push. They gave him space, hoping he would come around.

But something had shifted. The trio that once felt invincible now seemed fragile, the bond they shared no longer as unshakeable as it once was.

One day, as they sat under the familiar tree in their favorite park, Naina looked over at Rohan, concern in her eyes.

"You've been quiet lately," she said softly.

Rohan forced a smile. *"Yeah, just been thinking a lot, I guess."*

Priya leaned in; her expression serious. *"You know we're here for you, right? No matter what?"*

Rohan nodded, his heart warming at their words. He knew they meant it; knew they would always care for him. But he also knew that things were changing—that they were growing, evolving, moving in different directions. And maybe that was okay. Maybe it was just part of life.

He let out a deep breath, finally feeling a sense of peace wash over him. It was okay to let things change. It was okay to let go of the past, even when it hurt.

Epilogue: A New Beginning

Rohan never forgot that Shivaratri. But instead of letting it define him, he chose to see it as a turning point. It taught him the value of cherishing the present and allowing the past to slip away. His friends, though distant in some ways, would always hold a place in his heart. Memories faded, but they were never truly lost.

Life, after all, was about change—about moving forward, even when the path was uncertain. And as Rohan continued on his journey, he carried that lesson with him, ready to face the future with an open heart.

-The Dead Man

Three

An Unopened Story

Some stories, you see, aren't meant to be told. They linger quietly, folded away in the corners of memory, untouched by time but still pulsing with unspoken words and unresolved feelings. This story isn't about anyone specific—at least not in a way that matters to the world. But for one person, a young boy navigating the awkward corridors of adolescence, it was everything. This was his unopened story.

In 2019, Raghav was in the 9th grade, a shy boy who never quite felt like he belonged. He wasn't lonely per se—he had friends, a small group with whom he shared quiet moments and occasional laughter—but there was something about him that kept him on the outskirts of life's grander celebrations. He wasn't the one people remembered after the school bell rang; he was the observer, the one who watched.

And then there was Meera.

She wasn't like the others. There was something ethereal about her—a quiet grace that moved effortlessly between spaces, drawing people to her without a single word. Meera wasn't loud or overly outgoing, but her mere presence felt magnetic to Raghav. For the first time in his life, he found himself obsessing over someone. It wasn't love, at least not in the way he had read about in books or heard in the songs his friends played during lunch breaks. No, this was something else—a deep yearning, an unexplainable pull to be near her, to know her, to be part of her world.

Raghav tried. He mustered up the courage—something foreign to him—to talk to her, to make her laugh, to find common ground. And for a time, it worked. Or at least, he thought it did. They spoke briefly between classes, exchanged small smiles across the school courtyard, and once, during a group activity, their hands brushed against each other. It wasn't much, but to Raghav, it was enough to fill the pages of his dreams.

But dreams, as they often do, have a cruel way of unraveling.

At first, it was subtle. Meera's replies became shorter. She didn't smile as often when he passed by her in the hallways. Then, the distance grew more obvious. She stopped acknowledging him altogether. Weeks passed, and every time their paths crossed, she acted as though they had never spoken at all—as if Raghav were just another face in the sea of students. No greetings, no small talk, no familiar smile. Just… nothing.

Raghav was devastated but said nothing. He was an introvert, after all, and confrontation wasn't his style. He convinced himself that it must have been something he did, though he couldn't quite pinpoint what. Maybe he had laughed at the wrong time or said something awkward. Maybe she had simply moved on, found someone more interesting, more charismatic. He never asked, never sought clarity. He just let the silence grow between them until it became unbearable.

He stopped trying after that. The hurt was too much, and the fear of rejection too great. Raghav watched from afar, though, never able to fully let her go. Meera remained a constant thought, an obsession he couldn't explain. No matter how much time passed, no matter how many new friends he made, she held a place in his mind that no one else could fill. He didn't understand it, didn't try to. Some feelings just are.

Years passed, and Raghav buried those memories under layers of new experiences. School ended, life moved forward, and Meera faded into the background like a half-forgotten dream. But she was never completely gone. Every now and then, when Raghav allowed his mind to drift, he thought about her—wondered what could have been if things had played out differently, if he had been braver, if he had asked her what had happened between them. But those were questions left unanswered, buried in the unopened chapter of his life.

Then came 2024, and with it, an unexpected turn of fate.

Raghav hadn't thought much about Meera in the years since school, but one afternoon at a local Gurudwara, he saw her again. Time had passed, but she was just as he remembered, perhaps even more beautiful in the soft, serene light of the prayer hall. There she was, standing only a few feet away, talking to someone. Before he could decide what to do, Meera noticed him. This time, instead of ignoring him like she had all those years ago, she smiled. Not just a polite, passing smile, but a genuine one, filled with recognition and warmth.

It was as though the years between them had melted away.

"*Raghav?*" she asked, her voice laced with pleasant surprise.

Caught off guard, he stammered a greeting, feeling his heart pound in his chest. And just like that, they began talking again. The conversation was light at first, filled with the usual catching-up questions: *"What have you been up to?" "Where are you studying now?" "Do you come here often?"*

As the weeks went by, they kept running into each other—at events, during gatherings, at the Gurudwara. Each time, they talked a little more, the awkwardness of their past slowly fading into the background. But as much as Raghav enjoyed these moments, one question continued to gnaw at him: why had Meera pulled away all those years ago?

He never asked. He couldn't.

Every time the conversation edged toward something more personal, he steered it back to safer topics. Maybe, deep down, he didn't want to know. Maybe it was easier to leave that chapter unopened, to keep the mystery alive rather than risk uncovering something that could hurt him all over again. Perhaps it was better to remember the Meera of his youth, the girl who had captivated him, rather than face the truth of what had really happened. Raghav never asked for her phone number, never tried to extend their conversations beyond the confines of the Gurudwara. It was as though some invisible boundary existed between them—one he was too afraid to cross. He didn't want to break the fragile peace they had found, didn't want to risk losing her again, even if they were no longer the same people they had been. And so, Meera remained an unopened story, one that Raghav chose to keep tucked away, safe from the prying hands of reality. He heard things about her from others—whispers of negative gossip, things that painted her in a less-than-flattering light. But Raghav never believed them. He refused to let the world's version of Meera taint the image he had of her. In his mind, she would always remain that same ethereal girl from 9th grade—the girl he had once been obsessed with and perhaps still was, though he would never admit it. Some stories, Raghav realized, were better left unopened. They were meant to be preserved in memory, untouched and unspoiled. Meera was one of those stories for him. He might never pursue a friendship with her again, might never ask her why she had changed so suddenly all those years ago. But she would always hold a place in his heart—an unopened chapter, frozen in time.

And maybe, just maybe, that was enough.

-The Dead Man

Four

Fading Echoes

Part I: The Spark of Friendship

They say that the bonds we form in childhood are unbreakable, forged in the fires of innocence and adventure. For Maya and Arjun, this sentiment held true. Their story began on the first day of kindergarten, where the world felt vast and intimidating. Both children were shy, clinging to their mothers' sides as they took their first tentative steps into a new environment. But fate, it seemed, had a plan. Seated next to each other, they quickly discovered the power of shared crayons and whispered secrets, and from that moment, a friendship blossomed.

As the days turned into weeks, Maya and Arjun became

inseparable. Their laughter echoed in the playground as they explored every corner of their small town, turning mundane afternoons into epic adventures. Arjun, the quieter of the two, found balance in Maya's exuberance. She was loud and fearless, always pulling him into new escapades, encouraging him to step out of his shell. Their bond was pure, a friendship so deep that even as they grew older, they never seemed to outgrow each other.

With dreams as vast as the sky, they made promises that echoed through the years. Maya aspired to be an artist, her sketches a reflection of her vibrant imagination, while Arjun nurtured a passion for storytelling. They spent countless afternoons under their favorite oak tree, Maya pouring her heart into her drawings while Arjun spun tales around her art. Their worlds intertwined seamlessly, and they vowed that no matter where life took them, they would always be best friends.

Part II: The First Signs

Years passed, and with them came the winds of change. As high school approached, their lives began to diverge. Arjun set off to study literature in a distant city, while Maya stayed behind, fervently working towards a career in graphic design. Yet, despite the physical distance, their connection remained strong. Late-night calls and endless text messages kept them tethered to each other, while holiday reunions filled the gaps of separation.

However, during one particularly frosty winter break, a

subtle shift in Maya's demeanor began to trouble Arjun. *"Hey, remember our trip to the old lighthouse last summer?"* he casually asked one evening, a fond smile on his face as he recalled their thrilling late-night climb to watch the sunrise.

Maya paused, her brow furrowing in confusion. *"Lighthouse? I don't think I remember that..."*

Arjun chuckled, dismissing her uncertainty as a joke. *"Come on, you're not serious, are you? We almost got caught by the guard!"*

But Maya's expression remained unchanged—a mixture of confusion and a gentle smile that seemed to say she truly didn't recall. A pang of unease gripped Arjun, but he brushed it aside, convincing himself that it was merely a lapse in memory. After all, people forget things all the time.

Yet, as the months rolled on, it became apparent that this wasn't an isolated incident. Maya began to forget more and more—important things, cherished memories. Birthdays, plans they had made, the places they had explored together. Initially, these were minor details that seemed inconsequential, but gradually, the memories that formed the foundation of their friendship began to slip through the cracks, like sand through fingers. Arjun found himself feeling increasingly helpless.

"It's probably just stress," he reassured himself, trying to stave off the growing sense of dread. "She's juggling so much with school and work." But deep down, a voice whispered that something was terribly wrong.

Part III: The Diagnosis

One fateful day, a call from Maya's mother shattered Arjun's world. Her voice trembled, heavy with unspoken fears, as she revealed the devastating news: Maya had been diagnosed with early-onset Alzheimer's disease. The irony of it all struck Arjun like a thunderbolt—a vibrant girl with a brilliant future ahead was slowly being stolen away by a cruel twist of fate.

Sitting alone in his dorm room, the walls closing in around him, he struggled to comprehend the enormity of what he had just heard. The girl who had been his anchor, his constant source of joy and laughter, was fading away, and there was nothing he could do to stop it. Anger bubbled within him; he wanted to scream, to cry, to lash out at the universe for being so unfair. Instead, he felt an overwhelming, hollow sadness that wrapped around him like a shroud.

In the following weeks, Arjun dedicated himself to being a source of strength for Maya. He visited her as often as he could, determined to create new memories even as the old ones vanished like smoke. They would sit beneath their oak tree, just as they had during their childhood, but now a heaviness hung in the air, thick with the unspoken words they could no longer share.

One afternoon, as they sat in the dappled sunlight, Maya turned to Arjun, her eyes clouded with confusion. *"I know we're close, but I... I don't remember how we met. Can you tell me?"*

The question struck Arjun like a physical blow. His best friend, his other half, didn't recall their beginning. He forced a smile, fighting back tears as he swallowed the lump in his throat. *"Of course,"* he said softly, recounting the story of a little girl and boy, two shy souls who had found friendship over crayons and coloring books.

Maya listened intently, though her expression remained distant, as if she were desperately trying to grasp the fragments of a life she could no longer hold onto. When he finished, she offered a sad, knowing smile that pierced Arjun's heart. *"I wish I could remember,"* she whispered, and the weight of those words lingered in the air like a haunting melody.

Part IV: Holding on to Hope

As the months slipped by, Maya's condition continued to deteriorate. The familiar sparkle in her eyes dulled, replaced by uncertainty and fear. On her worst days, she would look at Arjun with a blank stare, not recognizing the boy who had been her companion through life's ups and downs. Each time this happened, a part of Arjun broke, the pain seeping into his very bones.

But even in the face of despair, he refused to give up. He began writing down their shared memories, crafting stories from their past—tales of laughter, adventure, and unwavering love. He filled notebooks with recollections of their childhood escapades, their dreams, and the promises they had made to one another. Each visit became a sacred ritual; he would read to Maya, hoping that maybe, just maybe, something would resonate within her.

One day, as he read a story filled with joy, Maya took his hand, her fingers trembling. *"I don't remember everything,"* she said slowly, searching his eyes, *"but I know I love you, Arjun. That's something I don't think I could ever forget."*

Tears welled in Arjun's eyes as he squeezed her hand tightly, his voice thick with emotion. *"I love you too, Maya. Always."*

Part V: The Final Goodbye

Inevitably, the day came when Maya could no longer recognize Arjun. Sitting by her side, he held her hand, feeling the warmth slowly slipping away, like the last rays of sunlight at dusk. She looked at him with vacant eyes, devoid of recognition. His heart shattered into a million pieces, but he remained steadfast, whispering stories of their past, desperately clinging to the fragments of who she once was.

Even as Maya's memories faded, Arjun refused to forget her. He continued to visit, to sit with her under their oak tree, recounting the life they had built together, always hoping to spark a flicker of recognition. But as time drew closer to its end, he understood that their shared history was slipping away like sand through an hourglass.

Then, one quiet evening, as the sun painted the sky in hues of orange and purple, Maya took her final breath. Arjun sat beside her, holding her hand until it turned cold, his tears falling silently. In that moment, he knew a part of him had died with her—the part that held their memories, the laughter, and the dreams they had woven together. But he also understood that she was finally at peace.

Epilogue: Remembering for Two

In the days that followed, Arjun immersed himself in writing. He filled page after page with the memories of a girl who had once been his entire world. He penned their adventures, their dreams, and the bond they had shared, writing not just for himself but for Maya, too. His heart found a new purpose: to remember for both of them, to keep their story alive.

As he wrote, he felt her presence beside him, a gentle whisper in the rustle of the leaves, a warm breeze that caressed his cheek. Though Maya was gone, their friendship, their love, would endure in the stories he crafted, a testament to a bond that not even time could erase.

Fading Echoes is a tale of friendship, loss, hope, and resilience. It serves as a poignant reminder that even as we lose the people we cherish, their impact on our lives is never truly gone. Sometimes, holding onto that impact is the most powerful way to honor those we love.

-The Dead Man

Five

The Whispers of a Dying Heart

The journey of life is something no one can truly prepare for. It's a road filled with detours, mistakes, and choices that sometimes lead to dead ends. For some, the ride is easy; for others, it's nothing short of a battle. And then there are those who look back, wondering if they could have done something differently, if they could have chosen a different path to avoid the wreckage, they now call their past.

He was one of those. The kind of person who had always seemed to be running—running from his fears, from the pain he carried, from the reality that life wasn't meant to be lived alone. But in his haste to escape, he lost so many people along the way.

In his youth, he had friends—so many of them. They were the ones who made life feel like a series of little adventures, shared laughs, and comforting words during hard times. There was a time when he believed he had everything he needed: friends who cared, a love that felt real, a future that felt full of endless possibilities.

But somewhere along the way, he started pushing people away. Maybe it was the fear of getting hurt again, or maybe it was his inability to communicate how he truly felt. He wasn't sure, but he knew it had started small. A harsh word here, an unforgiving glance there, a lie he didn't have the courage to take back. And then, slowly, but surely, the people who once filled his world began to slip away. At first, it didn't hurt. At first, he told himself they were the problem, not him. But as time passed, something started to change within him.

Years went by, and he watched as faces that had once been so familiar became distant memories. His friends—those who had once stood by his side—were gone. Some had drifted, their lives taking them in different directions, while others had simply had enough of his indifference, his inability to show them the love they had given him. And then there was her—his first love. The girl who had once made his heart race, who had shown him what it meant to truly care for someone, to give all of yourself to another person.

But even she had left.

He hadn't meant to hurt her, not really. But sometimes, when you don't know how to express yourself, you make the worst choices. You push people away when all you really want is for them to stay.

And now, at the age of 22, he was alone.

Alone in a world that once felt so full. Alone with a heart full of regret, a mind constantly replaying the moments he could've changed, the words he should've said, the actions he could've taken to hold on to what was precious to him.

Every person he had lost—whether a friend, a companion, or a lover—had left a scar. And these scars, though they never fully healed, slowly became part of him. They were like ghosts that followed him through life, haunting his every step, every choice, every decision he made.

But it wasn't just the people who had left that bothered him. It was the realization that he had allowed it to happen. That he had somehow failed, not only them but also himself. Because what was life without connection? What was love without the courage to hold on to it? What was friendship if you didn't nurture it, if you didn't fight for it?

As the years passed, his loneliness grew. It wasn't the kind of loneliness that came from physical distance. No, it was deeper. It was the kind that filled the spaces in his heart, the kind that reminded him every day that he had failed, that he had lost the most important thing in life: the people who mattered.

There were times, especially late at night, when the weight of it all became too much to bear. He would lay in bed, staring at the ceiling, wondering how it had all gone wrong. Was he really that bad at relationships? Was he too selfish, too proud, too afraid? Or was he simply doomed to live a life of endless regret?

But despite all the pain, despite all the tears he had shed in silence, there was something else he couldn't ignore. A tiny flicker of hope.

It wasn't hope for the past to change—that was long gone. It was hope for the future.

Maybe, just maybe, if he could understand what went wrong, he could fix it. Maybe if he learned to open up, to love without fear, to express his feelings without hiding behind walls of pride, he could salvage what was left. Maybe he could still find a way to hold on to people who mattered.

But deep down, he knew it wasn't going to be easy. He had spent so much of his life pushing people away, keeping them at arm's length, that it felt impossible to let them in again. But that didn't mean he wasn't willing to try.

And that's where the true challenge lay. Not in wishing for what he had lost, but in learning to move forward, in learning how to live without being constantly haunted by the ghost of the past.

He had learned, after all, that living was more than just existing. It was about finding peace with your mistakes, acknowledging your failures, and still having the strength to move forward. To love again. To trust again. To hope again.

And so, with every passing day, he made a choice. A choice to let go of the past—not to forget it, because it would always be a part of him—but to stop allowing it to control his future. A choice to embrace the idea that while life may be fleeting, love, in all its forms, was worth the effort. Even if it meant facing the fear of loss, even if it meant failing again.

Because in the end, the only thing worse than losing love was never having the courage to love at all.

So, he kept living, one day at a time, carrying the weight of his past, but choosing to let go of the guilt, the regret, and the fear. He wasn't perfect. He never would be. But he was learning. Learning to live with the dying, and to cherish the moments that still remained.

And maybe, just maybe, he could hold on to something real this time.

-The Dead Man

Six

The Unspoken Distance

There's a certain type of silence that builds over time. It starts in the smallest moments—tiny, unnoticed instances where words are left unsaid. You don't even see it coming. And by the time you do, it's already too late.

He couldn't exactly pinpoint the moment it began, but maybe it was that day. The day when his best friend didn't ask him if he was okay, didn't follow up with the usual questions. That day—an ordinary day for most, but one that would remain carved into his mind like an echo of something he didn't understand.

They had always been close. They had their inside jokes, their shared dreams, their stupid fights that never lasted more than a few days. And yet, on that day, the silence between them seemed louder than ever before.

He had gone to their usual coaching class, unaware of the holiday, only to find the doors locked and the hallways eerily empty. A small mistake, really. Nothing major. But when he called her, and she casually mentioned she had forgotten to tell him, something shifted.

She had told someone else. Someone new in her life.

It wasn't jealousy. No, it was more of a dull ache, a quiet realization that maybe she had started to move on without him. Maybe, just maybe, he wasn't as important to her as he used to be.

He didn't say anything. He couldn't. His pride wouldn't allow him to sound so… desperate. So instead, he sat outside the coaching center alone, his phone clenched in his hand, willing her to call back and say something more, something that would erase the gnawing feeling in his chest.

But the call never came.

Days turned into weeks, and although they still talked, something was missing. The small gestures, the little reassurances, the way she used to ask if he was okay when he was too stubborn to admit he wasn't—those were gone. And slowly, ever so slowly, the silence between them grew.

He blamed himself for it. Maybe if he hadn't been so proud, so caught up in his own hurt, things would've been different. Maybe if he had just said something, told her how much it hurt that she didn't tell him about the holiday, they could've laughed about it, moved on. But he stayed quiet, and the distance grew.

It wasn't just her. Over the years, he had let so many people slip away. Friends, companions, lovers—they all faded into the background, until all that was left was a memory of what once was. Sometimes it was his fault; sometimes it was theirs. But the result was always the same. He was left alone, standing on the edge of something that had once been beautiful, now nothing more than a series of missed opportunities and unsaid words.

And now, as he sat with his thoughts, he wondered if it had always been this way. If he had been destined to lose everyone, one by one, until all he had were memories of a time when he wasn't alone.

There was a letter he had written, one that he never sent. It was meant for her—his best friend, the one who had been with him through everything. The one who had taught him how to laugh, how to care, how to love.

He had written it late one night, the words spilling out of him like a dam had broken. He had been so angry, so hurt. But he couldn't bring himself to send it. Not because he didn't mean it, but because he was afraid. Afraid that if he said those words, it would be the end of everything.

And now, he wondered if it would've made a difference. If he had told her how much she meant to him, would she have stayed? Or was she already too far gone, lost to the same silence that had taken so many others?

He kept the letter in his phone, buried deep in his notes. He could never delete it. It was the only thing left of a friendship that had once been everything to him.

But even now, after all this time, he couldn't bring himself to send it. He knew it wouldn't change anything. It was too late for that.

The silence had already won.

-The Dead Man

Seven

The Last Breath of Silence

Raghav carried his secret like a heavy stone in his chest. For years, he lived in the shadow of it—his heart closed, his words guarded. He had learned to let silence fill the spaces where truth should be. It was easier to pretend nothing was wrong, easier to shut everyone out.

But the weight of unspoken words grew heavier with time. His mind wandered to the letter he had once written but never sent, words meant for his best friends—Anaya, and Riya. He had poured everything into that letter: his anger, his confusion, the frustration of being left behind. He had questioned their friendship, their intentions, his own worth. But in the end, he chose silence. Why disturb them when they seemed so happy? Why drag them into the storm he had created for himself?

The truth was, Raghav didn't know how to express what was

buried inside. Every time he tried to take a step forward, doubts consumed him. Maybe it was his fault they had drifted apart? Or maybe it wasn't worth the effort to reach out anymore? His mind circled back to the same unanswered questions, like a loop he couldn't escape.

It wasn't until he met Meera that something inside him began to change. She was quiet in a way that drew him in, a girl who seemed to carry her own silent burdens. They found each other in the middle of their loneliness, two people too scared to speak their truths. But there was a connection between them, one that didn't need words at first.

As their friendship grew, so did the unspoken understanding that they were both hiding from something. Meera wasn't afraid of silence—she embraced it, let it fill the room until it became comfortable. Raghav, on the other hand, felt the pressure build every time they sat together, the weight of all the things he had never said. But she never asked. And maybe that was why he was drawn to her—because Meera didn't expect answers.

One evening, as they sat on the rooftop under a blanket of stars, Raghav finally broke.

"Do you ever feel like you're drowning in your own thoughts?" he asked, his voice barely above a whisper.

Meera didn't look at him. She continued gazing at the sky, her arms wrapped around her knees. *"Every day."* She spoke.

Raghav's chest tightened. *"I wrote a letter once. I never sent it. To my best friends."* His words felt strange, as if they didn't belong to him. But once they were out, he couldn't stop. *"I thought I'd feel better writing it all down, but it only made everything worse. They were living their lives, happy, while I was stuck here... in my head, with all these stupid questions."*

Meera unfolds the letter and started reading, maybe she knows what's written in that letter, but she was still nervous, or maybe…just nothing? She started reading in her mind.

"To My Best Friend,

Sometimes, I wonder what I'm even doing. One moment, I unfollow you all, then out of nowhere, I get angry. Some days, I don't talk to you for weeks, and other times, I post stories with someone else just to make a point. There are moments when I think about letting go, moving on. But then, I remind myself that most of the mistakes were mine. And yet, I wonder—did any of you even try? But then again, did I ever make the first move?

There are so many questions in my head, so many things I want to say. But whenever I try to find answers, I'm just left with silence and loneliness. Sometimes, I think about meeting Aarav, Anaya, and Riya, and just letting out all the anger, hatred, and hurt I've been keeping inside. But then, I stop. Why should I disturb your peace when you all seem so happy? Every day, you're out there, going places, enjoying life, so why should I trouble you? Besides, I don't even have the time to deal with all this anymore. But then, new thoughts creep in.

All day, my mind fills with thousands of thoughts. A few of them are good, but most are bad. And standing in the middle of those thoughts, I wonder how different life would be if things were easier. How different would it be if expressing emotions were just a little easier than keeping them hidden? What would it be like if I could tell you all these things as easily as I'm writing them now? Is it really that hard to understand each other or to give people the chance to understand us? Maybe it is, maybe it isn't. But then I ask myself, does it even matter? Does it matter if you understand how I feel? What if you just laughed it off and didn't take it seriously?

Maybe I had a chance once, a chance to take that step forward. But now, it feels like that chance is gone. So many questions still flood my mind. But if I sat down to write them all, I might still be writing until morning. And even if I tried to pour a year's worth of anger onto a single page, how could I? I don't have enough time anymore, nor enough emotions to feel it all. Life's gotten busy for me, for you, and for them too.

It wasn't as hard as I thought it would be. And besides, with my short-term memory, it's possible that one day I'll forget all of this completely. Some people find it easy to hold onto memories, but maybe that's not so easy for me."

Meera turned to him then, her eyes soft but filled with something unspoken, like she understood exactly what he meant. *"What did you want from them?"*

Raghav laughed bitterly. *"I don't even know. An explanation? An apology? Maybe just... a sign that they cared. But I never asked them for any of it. I just kept expecting."*

"Expectations kill more than silence does," Meera said softly.

Her words hit him hard. All this time, he had been waiting for them to notice his pain, but he had never given them a chance to. Silence had become his shield, and it had also become his prison. He looked at Meera, realizing that she, too, had her own fortress of silence, and maybe that's why they understood each other so well.

Days turned into weeks, and the connection between them deepened. They still didn't speak much about the past, but the comfort of their presence spoke volumes. Until one day, Meera gave him a letter.

"I wrote this a long time ago," she said, her voice barely audible. *"I never gave it to the person it was meant for. But I think it's time I let go."*

Raghav took the letter, understanding immediately. He unfolded the page and read the words that mirrored his own unsent letter. It was a message to someone she had lost touch with; someone she had never forgiven—neither them nor herself.

"Dear You,

There are so many things I wish I had said to you, but I never could. I didn't know how, and maybe I was too afraid. Afraid that the words wouldn't come out right, afraid that you wouldn't understand. And in the end, I stayed silent—thinking that was easier. But now I'm not so sure.

There were moments when I thought you saw me, really saw me, and understood. But as time passed, it became clear that I had hoped for too much. I wanted you to reach out, to ask if I was okay, to notice when I was falling apart. But you never did. Maybe you were too busy, or maybe I was too good at hiding my pain.

I blamed you for not being there. I hated you for moving on when I couldn't. And I hated myself even more for still caring, for waiting for a sign that never came. Every time I saw you laugh, every time I saw you happy without me, it felt like a punch to the gut. And I told myself I didn't need you—I didn't need anyone. But that was a lie. The truth is, I needed you more than I ever wanted to admit.

But now I realize, you couldn't read my mind. You couldn't know what I never said. And I'm not sure if it would have made any difference if I had told you, but at least I wouldn't have been left with this aching silence between us.

So, here's what I wanted to say all this time: I was hurting. I was angry. I felt forgotten. But most of all, I missed you. I missed us. And I hated that I couldn't just tell you that.

Now, it's too late. I think we both know that. Too much has changed, and too much has been left unsaid. But still, I hold on to these words, hoping that somehow, somewhere, you might understand what I was never brave enough to say.

I wish you well, and I hope you find the happiness I couldn't give you.

Meera"

The letter was raw, filled with pain and questions, much like his own. And in that moment, Raghav realized that silence wasn't the answer. It never had been. The things they had kept buried were tearing them apart from the inside, and the only way to heal was to release them.

"I think... it's time I let go too," Raghav said, his voice trembling as he reached into his bag and pulled out the letter, he had written all those years ago.

Together, they unfolded the stories they had kept hidden for too long. And as the words spilled out, so did the pain. But along with the pain came something else—relief.

For the first time in years, Raghav felt like he could breathe again. The weight was lifting.

Silence had once been his only companion, but now, with Meera by his side, he realized that sharing his burden didn't make him weak—it made him human.

In the end, the silence that had once suffocated him gave way to the breath of life, and with it, the chance for both of them to finally heal.

-The Dead Man

Eight

The Unsent Letter

He sat alone in his room, staring at the screen of his phone. The room was dimly lit, casting shadows that flickered and danced like ghosts of forgotten moments. He scrolled through endless chats, reading messages that were now just remnants of something more—something he feared was gone forever.

There was a time when they were inseparable. Best friends, companions, partners in crime. Their bond was built on unspoken understanding, laughter shared over the smallest things, and secrets traded under a sky full of stars. They weren't just friends; they were each other's world.

But something had changed. He wasn't sure when or how, but he felt it. The distance. It wasn't physical, no. They were still a call away, still just a message apart. Yet, every interaction felt like a shadow of what it used to be. He tried to trace the moment when things started to unravel, but it was like trying to catch smoke—always slipping through his fingers.

He sighed, remembering that day. A day that should have been insignificant to anyone else, but to him, it had become a mark on his soul. He had gone to their usual hangout, excited to meet them, only to find the place deserted. A call later, he learned that they had all known about the holiday—everyone but him. And it wasn't the fact that they hadn't told him that hurt the most. It was that she hadn't told him. The one person who knew him inside out, who had always been the first to share every little thing. This time, she hadn't.

He couldn't explain why it hurt so much. Maybe it wasn't about that day at all. Maybe it was everything that had built up inside him. The little moments he had brushed off, the silences he had ignored, the words left unsaid. They had all started to weigh on him, like invisible bricks forming a wall between them.

He had wanted to talk to her that day, to ask why she hadn't told him, to share the hurt he was feeling. But instead, he stayed silent. He had told himself that it wasn't a big deal, that he didn't want to make her feel bad. But deep down, he knew the truth. He was scared. Scared that saying something would push her away. Scared that he'd lose her.

Days turned into weeks, and the silence between them grew louder. She had asked him once or twice if something was wrong, and he had brushed it off with a smile that didn't reach his eyes. He could've spoken then. But he didn't. He couldn't.

And now, sitting alone in his room, he realized that the distance between them had become too wide to cross. He had lost her, slowly but surely, not because of a single mistake, but because of all the moments he let slip by without saying a word.

He picked up his phone and typed a message, the words spilling out as if they had been waiting all this time. He wrote about the anger, the sadness, the regret. He told her how much he missed their friendship, how much he loved her, even if he could never say it out loud.

He re-read the message, his heart heavy with every word. For a moment, he hovered over the send button. But then, he locked his phone and let out a breath he didn't realize he was holding.

"I can't send it," he whispered to himself. *"Not now. Not ever."*

The message remained unsent, just like the thousands of thoughts he had kept inside over the years. Maybe one day, he would find the courage to tell her how much she meant to him. Maybe one day, he would explain why he hadn't spoken up when he should have.

But for now, the words would stay locked away, just like his heart.

He stood up, looking out of the window at the night sky. The stars were out, just like they had been when they used to talk for hours. The world outside moved on, oblivious to the storm raging inside him.

He had lost people before. Friends who had drifted away, lovers who had left, even family who had grown distant. But losing her felt different. It felt like losing a part of himself. Yet, in that loss, he had found something else—an understanding. Not everything could be fixed. Some things, some people, were meant to remain as memories, beautiful but unreachable.

And so, he let her go. Not with anger or regret, but with a quiet acceptance. She had been his world, and now, she was a chapter in his story—one that he would never forget, even if the words remained unsaid.

-The Dead Man

Nine

Afterword: The Weight of Stories Last Message for Reader

As you close this book, I want to thank you for taking the time to walk alongside the characters of Living with Dying. These stories were born not just from my imagination, but from a deeply personal place of reflection, pain, and hope. Writing them felt like opening a window into the quiet corners of my own heart—corners that I thought were forgotten but never truly were.

In life, we all grapple with loss, heartbreak, and the uncertainty of our existence. At times, these emotions feel overwhelming, like waves crashing against the fragile walls of our being. Yet, these stories remind us that even in our darkest moments, there is a flicker of light, a whisper of hope.

I hope these tales gave you something to hold on to—a memory, a feeling, or even a lesson. Perhaps you saw a piece of yourself in Rohan, who yearned for the simplicity of old friendships, or in Raghav, who grappled with the unanswered questions of love. Maybe Maya and Arjun reminded you of someone you've loved and lost, someone whose presence still lingers in your heart.

But beyond the characters and their struggles, this book is about you—the reader. It's about how you see your own story through theirs. Life often feels like a collection of unfinished sentences, a patchwork of emotions we try to make sense of. If this book has done anything, I hope it has given you permission to embrace those imperfections.

As a debut writer, this journey has been nothing short of surreal. From penning the first sentence to finally sharing it with you, every step was a leap of faith. I began writing Living with Dying as a way to make sense of my own emotions, but along the way, I realized how universal these feelings are.

To everyone who has ever faced the weight of grief, the sting of regret, or the bittersweet beauty of love—this book is for you.

I'd love to hear your thoughts, your interpretations, and even your criticisms. Stories, after all, live on through the people who read them, and I am grateful that you've allowed these tales to be a part of your journey.

Thank you for giving Living with Dying a place in your life.

With gratitude,
Ranveer Singh (The Dead Man)

About the Author

Ranveer Singh, writing under the pen name The Dead Man, is an emerging voice in emotional and introspective storytelling. His work explores the intricacies of human emotions, weaving together tales of love, loss, and resilience. Inspired by the delicate balance of life's joys and sorrows, his narratives resonate with readers on a deeply personal level.

Known for his poetic prose and vivid emotional landscapes, Ranveer aims to create stories that linger in the hearts and minds of his audience. "Living with Dying" is his debut collection, a testament to his belief in the enduring power of hope amidst life's challenges.

Ranveer's writing invites readers to reflect on their own journeys, connecting them with universal truths through the lens of poignant storytelling.

www.ingramcontent.com/pod-product-compliance
Ingram Content Group UK Ltd.
Pitfield, Milton Keynes, MK11 3LW, UK
UKHW040035200726
13845UKWH00054B/410

9 789334 327953